Series 401
A Ladybird Book

This delightfully illustrated story, told in verse, is about a mischievous squirrel called Bob Bushtail, and the adventure he gets into when he finds himself lost in the woods.

BOB BUSHTAIL'S ADVENTURE

Story and illustrations by A. J. MACGREGOR

Verses by W. PERRING

Ladybird Books Ltd Loughborough

Bobby Bushtail was a squirrel
   —And a naughty rascal, too—
Sometimes he was so untidy
   Mother didn't know what to do!

On the stool he'd stand and wriggle,
   When she tried to brush his tail,
And if she *combed* (a little crossly)
   He would even start to wail!

4

0 7214 0314 X

Baby Bushtail, Bobby's brother,

    Learned to climb and use his claws:

But, at first, was very nervous,

    Mother had to hold his paws!

When they had their nuts for breakfast,

　" I can't crack them ! " Baby said,

For his teeth were far too tiny :

　So Mother cracked them all instead.

One day, Mother said " Now children

    Gardening for you today !

Look, the garden's most untidy ;

    You must clear the weeds away !

Off they went, with tools on shoulders,

    Bob the rake and Jill the hoe;

Baby Bushtail had the basket,

    Into which the weeds would go.

How they bustled down the garden!

There the task they soon began:

Cleared away the weeds and grasses,

Made the pathway spick and span.

Bobby clambered up the palings,

    Gazed about with eager eyes:

Glancing downwards, how he started,

    Shouted out in pleased surprise!

There below him, big and tempting,

Acorns lay upon the ground!

" Jill ! " called Bobby, quite excited,

" Come and look what I have found ! "

Bobby, quick as thought, hopped over,

Broke off bits of wood until,

Panting, and a little tightly,

Through the gap squeezed Sister Jill!

Quite forgetting Mother's orders

Not to go outside the gate,

Off they scampered to the woodland !

What an acorn feast they ate !

Suddenly, around a tree-trunk,

    Baby saw, with startled eyes,

Open-jawed, a dog advancing,

    Filled the air with frightened cries!

Baby skipped away, and Shaggy
    (—Shaggy was the doggie's name)
Turned to Bobby for a playmate,
    —All he wanted was a game !

Bobby, though, was just as frightened,
    Scrambled higher up the tree !
Shaggy was a little puzzled,
    " Why will no-one play with me ? "

Meanwhile, Jill and Baby Bushtail

    Ran off homewards in their fright,

Scampered madly through the woodland,

    Quickly passing out of sight!

Shaggy, greatly disappointed,

Sadly watched them run away;

Thought " I don't think much of squirrels!

Went off somewhere else to play!

Shaggy vanished; Bobby saw him:

    Scurried quickly down the tree;

Noticed it was growing chilly,

    " We must hurry home ! " said he.

Through the wood in growing darkness,

   Bobby searched and searched again :

Called out " Jill ! " and " Baby ! *Baby* ! "

   But his cries were all in vain !

Now upon unhappy Bobby

Snow flakes fluttered thick and white;

So he found a hollow tree trunk;

Sheltered from the stormy night.

Here he lay and sobbed and shivered,

    While the wood grew white and dim:

Bobby thought of home and Mother,

    Thought they'd all forgotten him!

Meanwhile, back at '' Bushtail Cottage,''

   Jill and Baby, home once more,

Told their tale to Mrs. Bushtail,

   Waiting for them at the door!

" Well ! " said Mrs. Bushtail crossly,

   " Now you'll have no jam for tea ! "

As for Bobby, she was worried ;

   " Where," she thought, " can Bobby be ? "

Mr. Bushtail, rather grumpy

   And disturbed, said '' We must go

Back again and search the woodland,

   Lest he's buried in the snow ! ''

Softly through the silent woodland

    Went the lantern's bobbing light

Till they found him in his hollow,

    Curled up snugly, sleeping tight!

Underneath the big umbrella

    Back they bore the sleepyhead

" Never mind ! " said Daddy kindly,

    " Soon we'll have you safe in bed."

Once indoors, however, Bobby,
  By the fire, dry and warm,
While his Mother filled the tea-pot,
  Soon recovered from the storm :

Vowed he'd never more be naughty,
  Run off playing in the wood,
Disobeying Mother's orders :
  No ! In future, he'd be *good*.